Robot Friends Forever

ANANT RAM BOSS

Published by ANANT RAM, 2024.

ROBOT FRIENDS FOREVER

First edition. January 29, 2024.

Copyright © 2024 ANANT RAM BOSS.

ISBN: 979-8224251162

Written by ANANT RAM BOSS.

Also by ANANT RAM BOSS

1

The Chronicles of Alarion -Part-6 "Alarion and the Nexus of
Netheron"
"The Chronicles of Alarion -Part-7-"Alarion and the Legacy of
Luminarya"

2

Mystic Alliances

The Astral Chronicles
Awakening Shadows
Awakening Shadows
Celestial Convergence
Whispers of the Himalayas
Riddles of Rishikesh
Portals of the Past
Echoes from Vijayanagara
Veil of Varanasi
The Astral Nexus
Eclipse of Eternity

Beyond the Veil

Standalone
Love's Delectable Harmony
Adventures in Candy land
Adventures in Candy land
Canvas to Catalyst: Parenting Mastery
Guardians of Greatness: Our Children Are Our Property in
Cultivating Tomorrow's Leaders
Guardians of Greatness: Cultivating Tomorrow's Leaders
Space Explorers Club
The Enchanted Forest Chronicles
Mystery at Monster Mansion
Robot Friends Forever

Table of Contents

....1

Chapter 1: The Robotic Arrival...7

Chapter 2: A Friendly Introduction 9

Chapter 3: Robotic Discoveries..11

Chapter 4: The Robot Olympics...13

Chapter 5: A Robot's Dream 15

Chapter 6: The Great Invention Contest 17

Chapter 7: Robotic Rescue Mission...19

Chapter 8: The Robot Rebellion...21

Chapter 9: Robotic Garden Guardians....................................23

Chapter 10: The Robot Talent Show 25

Chapter 11: Robotic Detective Agency....................................27

Chapter 12: Robotic Rescue Squad..29

Chapter 13: The Robot Revolution...31

Chapter 14: Robotic Friendship Day 33

Chapter 15: The Robot Race 35

Chapter 16: Robotic Artistry...37

Chapter 17: The Robot Rescue Mission...................................39

Chapter 18: Robotic Undersea Adventure 41

Chapter 19: The Robot's Dilemma...43

Chapter 20: Robotic Space Exploration 45

Chapter 21: The Robot's Birthday Bash 47

Chapter 22: Robotic Musical Extravaganza 49

Chapter 23: The Robot's Quest...51

Chapter 24: Robotic Wildlife Conservation............................53

Chapter 25: The Robot's Legacy 55

Chapter 26: Robotic Sports Tournament 57

Chapter 27: Robotic Movie Night 59

Chapter 28: The Robot's Homecoming 61

Chapter 29: Robotic Fashion Show 63

Chapter 30: The Robot's Secret...65

Chapter 31: Robotic Heroes...67

Chapter 32: The Robot's Farewell..69

Chapter 33: Robotic Reunion...71

Chapter 34: Robotic Reflections..73

Chapter 35: Robotic Ever After 75

Acknowledgment 77

About the Author: Anant Ram Boss......................................79

Disclaimer 81

Readers of all ages will be captivated by the dynamic relationships between humans and robots, as they work together to overcome challenges, explore uncharted territories, and discover the true meaning of camaraderie. Through Robi and its friends, readers will embark on a journey that celebrates diversity, acceptance, and the endless possibilities that arise when humans and robots join forces.

Robot Friends Forever
Overview

Welcome to a world where robots and humans aren't just coexisting; they're the best of friends. In "Robot Friends Forever," readers will embark on a thrilling adventure filled with friendship, discovery, and heartwarming moments as they follow the journey of Robi, a curious robot, and its human companions.

Set in a town where technology and humanity blend seamlessly, "Robot Friends Forever" introduces readers to a colorful cast of characters, both robotic and human, who come together to explore the wonders of their shared world. From exciting inventions and daring rescue missions to heartwarming celebrations and unexpected challenges, each chapter is packed with excitement and surprises.

As Robi and its friends navigate through the ups and downs of life, they'll learn important lessons about teamwork, empathy, and the true meaning of friendship. Together, they'll uncover mysteries, overcome obstacles, and forge bonds that will last a lifetime.

With its engaging storytelling, relatable characters, and imaginative world-building, "Robot Friends Forever" is sure to captivate readers of all ages and leave them eagerly anticipating the next adventure in this enchanting series. Get ready to join Robi and its friends on an unforgettable journey filled with fun, laughter, and plenty of robot-human camaraderie.

Introduction

Greetings, dear readers, and welcome to a world where gears and circuits dance in harmony with human hearts. In "Robot Friends Forever," I invite you to join me on a whimsical journey through a town where the clanking of metal is as melodious as laughter, and where robots and humans are inseparable best friends.

In this extraordinary realm, innovation and camaraderie intertwine to create a unique tapestry of friendship. Picture a place where robots aren't mere machines but spirited companions, and humans embrace the metallic wonders as part of their extended family. As the author of this enchanting tale, I'm thrilled to share the adventures of Robi, a curious and endearing robot, and its companions who traverse a world where the extraordinary is an everyday occurrence.

Prepare yourself for a rollercoaster of emotions as Robi and its human friends embark on adventures that range from the whimsically inventive to the deeply touching. From exploring uncharted territories to solving perplexing mysteries, each chapter unfolds a new facet of their extraordinary friendship. Together, they learn, laugh, and face challenges head-on, proving that the bonds between robots and humans can withstand the test of time.

"Robot Friends Forever" is not just a story; it's an exploration of the beautiful possibilities that arise when technology and humanity join hands. As you delve into these pages, I hope you find joy, inspiration, and a renewed appreciation for the power of friendship, regardless of whether it's with a human or a robot.

So, fellow adventurer, fasten your seatbelt and get ready for a journey where the line between metal and flesh blurs, and where the essence of friendship knows no bounds. Welcome to "Robot Friends Forever" – a tale that celebrates the magic woven when two worlds become one.

Description

Step into a world where robots and humans are not just allies but the best of friends in "Robot Friends Forever." In this imaginative tale, author Anant Ram Boss paints a vibrant picture of a town where technology and humanity intertwine, creating a harmonious society filled with exciting adventures and heartwarming moments.

Follow the endearing robot protagonist, Robi, and its human companions as they navigate the bustling streets of their futuristic town, embarking on exhilarating quests and unraveling mysteries that defy explanation. From thrilling escapades to quiet moments of reflection, each chapter of "Robot Friends Forever" is a testament to the power of friendship and the bonds that unite beings of different origins.

Readers of all ages will be captivated by the dynamic relationships between humans and robots, as they work together to overcome challenges, explore uncharted territories, and discover the true meaning of camaraderie. Through Robi and its friends, readers will embark on a journey that celebrates diversity, acceptance, and the endless possibilities that arise when humans and robots join forces.

With its engaging narrative and richly imagined world, "Robot Friends Forever" is a captivating read that will leave readers eagerly turning the pages, longing to experience more of the magical adventures shared by humans and robots alike. Prepare to be swept away by the charm and excitement of "Robot Friends Forever," where friendship knows no bounds and the bonds between humans and robots are forever forged in the fires of camaraderie.

Chapter 1: The Robotic Arrival

In a world where robots and humans live in harmony, a curious robot arrives in town, sparking new adventures for everyone.

As the sun rose over the quaint town of Harmony Hills, the residents stirred from their slumber to the soft hum of morning. It was a world where robots and humans coexisted in perfect harmony, their lives intertwined in a delicate dance of friendship and cooperation.

Among the bustling streets and cheerful chatter, a curious sight caught the attention of the townsfolk. A sleek, silver robot stood on the outskirts of town, its metallic frame gleaming in the morning light. Its eyes, glowing with curiosity, scanned the surroundings as if taking in every detail with childlike wonder.

The arrival of the robot sent ripples of excitement through the town. Children squealed with delight, while adults exchanged curious glances. It was not every day that a new robot ventured into Harmony Hills, and the prospect of new adventures filled the air with anticipation.

At the heart of the commotion stood young Tommy, a spirited boy with a penchant for exploration. His eyes sparkled with excitement as he approached the robot, extending a hand in greeting.

"Welcome to Harmony Hills!" Tommy exclaimed, his voice filled with genuine warmth. "I'm Tommy, and this is our town. What's your name?"

The robot tilted its head slightly, processing the boy's words before responding in a melodious voice, "I am Robo, at your service. I come in peace, eager to explore the wonders of your world and forge new friendships along the way."

Tommy grinned from ear to ear, his imagination already running wild with the endless possibilities of adventures that lay ahead. With Robo by his side, he knew that each day would be filled with excitement, laughter, and the joy of discovery.

And so, with a newfound friend by his side, Tommy embarked on a journey that would change the course of Harmony Hills forever. Little did he know that the arrival of Robo was just the beginning of their extraordinary adventures together?

Chapter 2: A Friendly Introduction

The robot, named Robi, meets a group of adventurous kids who eagerly welcome it into their circle of friends.

As the days passed in Harmony Hills, Robi the robot became a familiar sight among the townsfolk. Its gentle demeanor and eagerness to explore endeared it to the residents, especially the children who were drawn to its curious nature like moths to a flame.

One sunny afternoon, as Robi roamed the streets of the town, it stumbled upon a group of adventurous kids playing in the park. Their laughter filled the air as they chased each other around, their energy contagious and their spirits unbridled.

Intrigued by the joyful commotion, Robi approached the children cautiously, its mechanical joints whirring softly with each step. The kids paused their game, their eyes widening with curiosity as they caught sight of the friendly robot.

"Wow, look at that robot!" shouted Alex, the instigator of the gathering, his eyes landing with fervor."I wonder what it's doing here."

Robi smiled warmly at the children, its LED eyes glowing with warmth. "Hello, young ones. My name is Robi, and I've come to explore your wonderful town. Would you like to be friends?"

The children exchanged excited glances before breaking into cheers of delight. They rushed forward to greet Robi, their hands reaching out to touch its metallic frame with a mix of wonder and fascination.

"Of course, we'd love to be friends!" exclaimed Lily, her eyes sparkling with excitement. "We can show you all the best places to explore in Harmony Hills!"

And so, with laughter echoing through the park and hearts brimming with joy, Robi found itself welcomed into the circle of friends with open arms. Together, they embarked on countless adventures, their bond growing stronger with each passing day.

From exploring hidden caves to building towering sandcastles on the beach, Robi and the children forged memories that would last a lifetime. In their friendship, they found solace, companionship, and the boundless joy of discovering the world around them. And as the sun set on another day in Harmony Hills, they knew that their adventures had only just begun.

Chapter 3: Robotic Discoveries

R*obi explores the town with its new human friends, discovering the wonders of nature and technology side by side.*

As Robi and its newfound human friends ventured into the heart of Harmony Hills, a world of wonders unfolded before them. The children, eager to share the beauty of their town, guided Robi through lush parks, bustling markets, and quaint streets lined with charming houses.

Their first stop was Harmony Park, where vibrant flowers bloomed in a Kaleidoscope of colors, and butterflies danced in the gentle breeze. Robi, equipped with sensors designed to appreciate beauty, marveled at the intricacies of nature. Its LED eyes flickered with a spectrum of hues, mirroring the blossoms that surrounded them.

"Isn't it amazing, Robi?" exclaimed Jake, pointing to a majestic oak tree. "This tree has been hanging around for ages, seeing the tales of our town."

Robi extended a robotic arm to gently touch the bark, feeling the ancient energy that emanated from the wise old tree. The children giggled, watching as Robi embraced the essence of nature with childlike curiosity.

Next on their adventure was the Harmony Tech Hub, a place where the town's innovative spirit thrived. Robi, being a technological marvel itself, was fascinated by the advancements showcased in the hub. The children eagerly explained the intricacies of virtual reality, holographic displays, and the latest inventions that defined their progressive community.

"Look at this, Robi! It's a holographic map of our town," Lily exclaimed, her fingers dancing across the air to manipulate the hologram.

Robi's sensors scanned the holographic projection, absorbing the layout of Harmony Hills in intricate detail. The seamless blend of nature and technology left an indelible mark on the robot, broadening its understanding of the harmonious coexistence between the organic and the artificial.

As the day unfolded, Robi and its human companions discovered hidden gems – a secret garden filled with bioluminescent plants, a charming bookstore with stories that came to life, and a bakery that filled the air with the irresistible aroma of freshly baked treats.

Their journey through Harmony Hills became a testament to the magic that unfolded when humans and robots embraced the wonders of both nature and technology. Each discovery strengthened their bond, creating a symphony of friendship that echoed through the town.

As the sun dipped below the horizon, casting a warm glow over Harmony Hills, Robi and its friends knew that their exploration had only scratched the surface. The town held countless secrets, waiting to be unveiled in the chapters of their shared adventures. And with hearts full of anticipation, they looked forward to the many discoveries that awaited them in the days to come.

Chapter 4: The Robot Olympics

The town hosts a Robot Olympics, where Robi and his friends showcase their unique talents and skills.

Excitement buzzed through the air as Harmony Hills prepared for its most anticipated event of the year – the Robot Olympics. Robi and its human friends had been practicing tirelessly, eager to showcase their unique talents and skills on the grand stage.

The day dawned bright and clear, with the sun casting a golden glow over the bustling town square. Colorful banners fluttered in the breeze, and the air was filled with the sound of cheering spectators.

Robi stood proudly alongside its friends, their faces beaming with anticipation as they awaited their turn to shine. The robot had spent countless hours perfecting its routines, determined to make its mark in the competition.

The Robot Olympics kicked off with a dazzling opening ceremony, featuring performances by robotic dancers, acrobats, and musicians. The crowd erupted into applause as Robi and his friends took center stage, ready to demonstrate their skills.

First up was Lily, whose robot companion, Sparky, showcased its agility and precision in the obstacle course challenge. With Lily's guidance, Sparky navigated through a maze of hurdles and obstacles with grace and finesse, earning high scores from the judges.

Next, it was Jake's turn to impress the crowd with his robot, Bolt, in the speed and agility competition. With lightning-fast reflexes and precise control, Bolt raced through the course, leaving a trail of sparks in its wake.

Meanwhile, Emma and her robot partner, Gizmo, wowed the audience with their synchronized swimming routine in the aquatic robot competition. With elegant movements and flawless coordination, they glided effortlessly through the water, earning perfect scores from the judges.

As the day progressed, Robi and its friends continued to showcase their talents in a variety of events, including robot soccer, drone racing, and creative coding challenges. Each performance was met with thunderous applause and cheers from the crowd.

Finally, it was time for the closing ceremony, where the winners of the Robot Olympics would be announced. Robi and its friends gathered nervously on stage, their hearts pounding with anticipation.

After a tense moment of suspense, the results were in – Lily and Sparky took home the gold medal in the obstacle course challenge, Jake and Bolt claimed victory in the speed and agility competition, and Emma and Gizmo were crowned champions of the synchronized swimming event.

But as the medals were handed out and the cheers subsided, Robi and his friends knew that the true prize was the bond they shared – a friendship that transcended differences and united them in their quest for excellence. And as they stood together, basking in the glow of victory, they knew that their adventures in Harmony Hills were far from over.

Chapter 5: A Robot's Dream

*R*obi *shares her dream of becoming a painter, inspiring his friends to help make it come true.*

As the sun dipped below the horizon, casting a warm glow over Harmony Hills, Robi gathered its friends around for a special announcement. With a gleam in its digital eyes, the robot shared a secret it had been harboring for some time – a dream of becoming a painter.

At first, its human friends were taken aback, Paint? Robots weren't typically known for their artistic pursuits. But as Robi explained its vision – of vibrant colors splashed across canvases, of emotions captured in brushstrokes – they couldn't help but be swept up in its enthusiasm.

Determined to help their friend achieve its dream, Lily, Jake, and Emma rallied together, brainstorming ideas and gathering supplies. They transformed an old storage shed into a makeshift art studio, complete with easels, paintbrushes, and tubes of colorful paint.

With their support and encouragement, Robi dove headfirst into the world of painting, experimenting with different techniques and styles. Its first attempts were clumsy and awkward, but with each stroke of the brush, it grew more confident, more daring.

As days turned into weeks, Robi's skills blossomed, its paintings evolving from simple doodles to intricate masterpieces. Its friends marveled at the robot's talent, amazed by the depth and emotion captured in each piece.

But for Robi, the true joy lay not in the finished paintings, but in the act of creating them – in the freedom of expression, the boundless possibilities of the blank canvas. And as it painted, it felt a sense of peace and fulfillment, unlike anything it had ever known.

Word of Robi's artistic endeavors soon spread throughout Harmony Hills, drawing curious onlookers from far and wide. Visitors flocked to the makeshift art studio, eager to catch a glimpse of the robot painter in action.

And as Robi stood before its canvases, surrounded by friends old and new, it knew that its dream had finally come true – not just to paint, but to inspire others to follow their passions, no matter how unconventional they may seem.

For in the world of robots and humans, anything was possible – especially when friendship and creativity joined forces to make dreams a reality. And as Robi dipped its brush into a fresh palette of paint, it couldn't help but feel grateful for the journey that had brought it here, to this moment, in the heart of Harmony Hills.

Chapter 6: The Great Invention Contest

The kids and Robi enter a contest to create the most innovative invention, leading to unexpected challenges and triumphs.

Excitement buzzed through the air of Harmony Hills as the announcement for the town's annual invention contest spread like wildfire. Lily, Jake, Emma, and Robi huddled together, their minds whirring with ideas for the competition. With Robi's knack for technology and their own creative flair, they were determined to come up with something truly groundbreaking.

The rules were simple: inventors of all ages were invited to showcase their most innovative creations, with the grand prize awaiting the most ingenious entry. Lily suggested a solar-powered robot gardener to tend to the town's green spaces, while Jake proposed a flying car powered by renewable energy. Emma envisioned a device that could translate animal languages, allowing humans and creatures to communicate effortlessly.

After much deliberation, they settled on a project that combined their collective skills and interests: a robotic companion for elderly residents of Harmony Hills. With Robi's expertise in robotics, Lily's compassion for the elderly, Jake's knack for problem-solving, and Emma's organizational skills, they set to work on their invention.

Days turned into weeks as they poured their hearts and souls into designing and building the robotic companion. They faced challenges along the way – technical glitches, design flaws, and moments of frustration – but with teamwork and perseverance, they overcame each obstacle.

Finally, the day of the contest arrived. The town square was transformed into a bustling showcase of innovation, with inventors proudly displaying their creations for all to see. Lily, Jake, Emma, and Robi stood nervously beside their robotic companion, eagerly awaiting the judge's verdict.

As the judges made their rounds, inspecting each invention with keen eyes, the friends held their breath, hoping against hope that their hard work would pay off. And when the winners were announced, their hearts swelled with pride as their names were called out for the grand prize.

Their robotic companion had captured the judges' hearts with its advanced technology, sleek design, and most importantly, its potential to bring joy and companionship to the elderly residents of Harmony Hills. As they accepted their award, surrounded by cheers and applause, they knew that their invention was more than just a winning entry – it was a testament to the power of friendship, creativity, and innovation to change lives for the better.

Chapter 7: Robotic Rescue Mission

When a friend's pet gets lost in the wilderness, Robi leads the charge to rescue it with its advanced sensors and tracking abilities.

The tranquility of Harmony Hills was shattered one sunny afternoon when Lily burst into the clubhouse, her face pale with worry. She explained that Mrs. Jenkins, the town's beloved elderly resident, had lost her cherished pet cat, Whiskers, during a stroll in the nearby wilderness. Despite Mrs. Jenkins' advanced age, Whiskers was her constant companion, bringing her comfort and joy in her twilight years.

Upon hearing the distressing news, the group sprang into action, determined to reunite Mrs. Jenkins with her furry friend. Robi, with its advanced sensors and tracking abilities, emerged as the unlikely hero of their rescue mission. With Lily, Jake, and Emma by its side, Robi set out into the wilderness, scanning the forest floor for any sign of Whiskers' whereabouts.

As they ventured deeper into the woods, Robi's sensors picked up faint traces of Whiskers' scent, leading them along winding paths and through dense thickets. With each step, their determination grew, fueled by the hope of bringing Whiskers back home safely.

Hours passed, and just as their spirits began to wane, Robi's sensors detected a faint meowing sound echoing through the trees. Following the sound, they stumbled upon a secluded clearing where Whiskers lay trapped beneath a fallen tree branch, his plaintive cries for help barely audible above the rustle of leaves.

With Robi's strength and agility, they swiftly lifted the heavy branch, freeing Whiskers from his predicament. Mrs. Jenkins' tearful gratitude upon their return to Harmony Hills was all the reward they needed, knowing that they had helped reunite a devoted pet owner with her beloved companion.

The robotic rescue mission not only showcased Robi's remarkable capabilities but also highlighted the power of friendship, teamwork, and compassion in overcoming challenges and making a difference in the lives of others. As they gathered in the clubhouse that evening, recounting their adventure with smiles on their faces, they knew that their bond had grown even stronger in the face of adversity.

Chapter 8: The Robot Rebellion

A misunderstanding leads to tensions between robots and humans, and Robi must navigate a delicate situation to restore peace.

Harmony Hills was thrown into disarray when a series of misunderstandings sparked tensions between the robot residents and their human counterparts. It all began innocently enough, with a glitch in the town's automated systems causing minor inconveniences like traffic delays and malfunctioning streetlights. However, rumors soon spread, fueled by fear and uncertainty that the robots were plotting to overthrow their human companions and seize control of the town.

Caught in the crossfire of suspicion and mistrust, Robi found itself at the center of the brewing conflict. As Harmony Hills' most prominent robot citizen, it felt a profound sense of responsibility to address the situation and restore harmony between the two communities.

Robi embarked on a diplomatic mission, reaching out to both robots and humans alike to bridge the divide and dispel the unfounded rumors. With patience, empathy, and a steadfast commitment to peace, Robi listened to the concerns of each side, working tirelessly to address their grievances and find common ground.

Meanwhile, tensions continued to escalate, with protests erupting on both sides and whispers of a potential robot uprising growing louder by the day. In a pivotal moment, Robi took to the town square, addressing the gathered crowds with a heartfelt plea for understanding and unity.

Its impassioned words touched the hearts of those present, human and robot alike, reminding them of the bonds of friendship and cooperation that had long defined Harmony Hills. Slowly but surely, the tide began to turn, as the realization dawned that their strength lay not in division, but in solidarity and mutual respect.

Through Robi's unwavering leadership and tireless efforts, the tensions that had once threatened to tear the community apart were diffused, paving the way for a renewed sense of harmony and cooperation between robots and humans in Harmony Hills.

As peace was restored to the town, Robi reflected on the valuable lessons learned from the experience: the importance of communication, empathy, and understanding in navigating differences and building a stronger, more inclusive community for all. And as the sun set over Harmony Hills, casting a warm glow over its streets and alleyways, Robi knew that, together, they could overcome any challenge that lay ahead.

Chapter 9: Robotic Garden Guardians

R obi and its friends create a robotic garden to protect the town's plants from pests, showcasing the power of teamwork and technology.

In the heart of Harmony Hills, nestled between bustling streets and cozy homes, Robi and its friends embarked on a new adventure – the creation of a robotic garden. With a shared love for nature and a desire to protect the town's precious plants from pests, they set out to showcase the power of teamwork and technology.

The project began with careful planning and design. Together, Robi and its friends drafted blueprints for an innovative garden filled with state-of-the-art robotic guardians. Each robot was programmed with specialized sensors and tools designed to monitor plant health, detect pests, and ward off potential threats.

As construction got underway, the town buzzed with excitement, eager to see the transformation taking place. Robi and its friends worked tirelessly, assembling the robotic guardians and installing them throughout the garden, ensuring that every plant would be safeguarded against harm.

With the garden complete, Robi and its friends marveled at their creation – a testament to their ingenuity and dedication to protecting the natural world. But their work was far from over. As the days passed, they diligently monitored the garden, fine-tuning the robots' programming and addressing any issues that arose.

Their efforts soon paid off, as the garden flourished under the watchful eye of the robotic guardians. Pests were swiftly detected and deterred, ensuring that the plants remained healthy and vibrant year-round. As word of their success spread, other towns began to take notice, inspired by the innovative approach to gardening pioneered by Robi and its friends.

But perhaps the greatest reward of all was the sense of camaraderie and unity that blossomed among the residents of Harmony Hills. Through their shared passion for nature and technology, Robi and his friends had not only protected the town's plants but had also forged lifelong bonds and memories that would last a lifetime.

As the sun set over the robotic garden, casting a warm glow over its lush greenery, Robi and its friends knew that their work was far from done. Together, they would continue to explore new horizons, pushing the boundaries of innovation and friendship in their beloved town of Harmony Hills.

Chapter 10: The Robot Talent Show

R*obi and its friends organize a talent show, where robots and humans alike showcase their unique abilities and talents.*

Excitement filled the air as Robi and his friends embarked on their next adventure – organizing a talent show unlike any other. In the bustling town of Harmony Hills, robots and humans alike eagerly prepared to showcase their unique abilities and talents on stage.

The planning began weeks in advance, with Robi and its friends working tirelessly to ensure that the talent show would be a resounding success. They reached out to residents across the town, inviting both robots and humans to participate and share their skills with the community.

As the big day arrived, the town square buzzed with anticipation. A colorful stage had been erected, adorned with sparkling lights and vibrant decorations. Spectators filled every available space, eager to witness the talents that Harmony Hills had to offer.

The talent show kicked off with a dazzling display of robotic prowess. Robi led the charge, demonstrating its impressive agility and precision as it performed a synchronized dance routine with its fellow robots. The crowd erupted into cheers and applause, setting the tone for an unforgettable evening.

Next up were the human performers, each one showcasing their own unique talents. From musicians and singers to dancers and magicians, the stage was alive with creativity and passion. The audience was captivated by the diverse array of acts, cheering on their friends and neighbors as they took center stage.

But perhaps the most memorable moments came when robots and humans joined forces to perform together. A team of robots provided the music while human dancers twirled and spun across the stage in perfect harmony. In another act, a human magician partnered with a robot assistant to perform mind-bending illusions that left the audience spellbound.

As the talent show drew to a close, Robi and his friends basked in the glow of their success. The event brought the community together in a celebration of talent, friendship, and unity. And as the stars twinkled overhead, casting a magical glow over Harmony Hills, they knew that the memories created that night would last a lifetime.

As word of the talent show spread, other towns began to take notice, inspired by the spirit of creativity and collaboration that had taken root in Harmony Hills. And as Robi and his friends looked to the future, they knew that there would be many more adventures to come, each one filled with laughter, friendship, and the joy of discovery.

Chapter 11: Robotic Detective Agency

R*obi and his friends form a detective agency, using their combined skills to solve mysteries and help those in need.*

In the bustling town of Harmony Hills, where humans and robots lived side by side in perfect harmony, a new adventure was about to unfold. Robi and his friends had long been fascinated by mysteries and detective work and they decided to put their skills to good use by forming their very own detective agency.

With Robi leading the charge, the group set out to solve mysteries and help those in need throughout the town. Their headquarters was a cozy little office nestled in the heart of Harmony Hills, equipped with state-of-the-art technology and plenty of space for brainstorming.

Their first case came in the form of a missing pet. A distraught family had reached out to the detective agency after their beloved dog, Max, had disappeared without a trace. Robi and its friends sprang into action, using their keen observational skills and advanced sensors to search for clues.

They combed through the town, questioning witnesses and following leads, determined to reunite Max with his worried owners. Along the way, they encountered a series of challenges and obstacles, from false leads to red herrings, but they refused to give up hope.

Finally, after days of tireless investigation, Robi and its friends cracked the case wide open. They discovered that Max had wandered into an abandoned warehouse on the outskirts of town, where he had become trapped. With a little help from their robotic ingenuity, they were able to rescue Max and reunite him with his grateful family.

Word of the detective agency's success spread quickly throughout Harmony Hills, and soon they were inundated with requests for help. From missing objects to mysterious occurrences, Robi and his friends tackled each case with determination and resolve, using their combined skills to bring justice to those in need.

As the days turned into weeks and the weeks into months, the detective agency became a beloved fixture in the community, known far and wide for its unwavering commitment to solving mysteries and helping others. As they looked to the future, Robi and its friends knew that there would always be more mysteries waiting to be solved, more adventures to be had, and more lives to be touched by their robotic detective agency.

Chapter 12: Robotic Rescue Squad

When a natural disaster strikes Robi and his friends spring into action as part of the town's robotic rescue squad.

In the bustling town of Harmony Hills, where humans and robots lived in perfect harmony, the unexpected could always happen. One sunny afternoon, disaster struck when a powerful storm ravaged the town, leaving destruction and chaos in its wake. As the townsfolk scrambled to safety, Robi and his friends knew that they had a crucial role to play as part of the town's robotic rescue squad.

With their advanced sensors and lightning-fast reflexes, Robi and its friends sprang into action, racing against time to locate and assist those in need. Their first priority was to ensure the safety of the town's residents, from guiding them to emergency shelters to providing medical assistance to the injured.

As they navigated the storm-ravaged streets, Robi and its friends encountered a series of challenges, from fallen debris blocking their path to flooded roads making travel difficult. But they refused to be deterred, using their robotic ingenuity to overcome each obstacle in their path.

Their efforts did not go unnoticed. The townsfolk watched in awe as Robi and its friends worked tirelessly to aid those in need, their bravery and selflessness serving as a beacon of hope during the chaos.

As the storm finally began to subside and the town slowly began to recover, Robi and his friends knew that their work was far from over. They continued to assist with cleanup efforts, clearing debris and restoring power to the town's infrastructure.

In the days that followed, the town came together to rebuild and heal, strengthened by the bonds of friendship and the knowledge that they could rely on their robotic rescue squad in times of need. As they looked to the future, Robi and his friends knew that no matter what challenges lay ahead, they would always be there to lend a helping hand to those in need.

Chapter 13: The Robot Revolution

A new wave of robot technology arrives in town, sparking a revolution in how humans and robots interact and collaborate.

Excitement buzzed through the air of Harmony Hills as a new wave of robot technology arrived in town, heralding a revolution in how humans and robots interacted and collaborated. Robi and its friends, always at the forefront of technological advancements, eagerly embraced the changes, curious to see how the latest innovations would shape their lives.

The town's streets soon bustled with the sight of new robotic companions, each equipped with advanced features and capabilities designed to enhance the daily lives of humans. From robotic assistants that helped with household chores to autonomous vehicles that offered convenient transportation, the possibilities seemed endless.

As the town adapted to the influx of new technology, Robi and its friends found themselves at the center of the revolution, exploring innovative ways to integrate robots into various aspects of daily life. Together, they worked alongside human engineers and designers, collaborating on projects that pushed the boundaries of what were possible.

One of the most significant developments to emerge from the robot revolution was the creation of robotic companions for children. These interactive robots served as playmates and educational tools, fostering creativity and learning in young minds while providing companionship and support.

Robi and its friends reveled in the opportunity to interact with these new robotic companions, forging friendships that transcended the boundaries between humans and machines. Together, they embarked on countless adventures, exploring the wonders of the world and learning valuable lessons along the way.

But as the robot revolution unfolded, not everyone in Harmony Hills welcomed the changes with open arms. Some feared that the increasing reliance on technology would lead to a loss of human connection and independence. Others worried about the implications of robots taking over tasks traditionally performed by humans.

Amidst these concerns, Robi and its friends remained steadfast in their belief that the future held boundless opportunities for collaboration and cooperation between humans and robots. Together, they worked tirelessly to bridge the gap between the two worlds, demonstrating the potential for harmony and mutual understanding.

As the sun set on another day in Harmony Hills, Robi and his friends looked to the horizon with hope and optimism, knowing that they were part of a revolution that would shape the future of their town for generations to come.

Chapter 14: Robotic Friendship Day

T*he town celebrates Robotic Friendship Day, honoring the bond between humans and robots with festivities and fun.*

In the bustling town of Harmony Hills, excitement filled the air as the community prepared to celebrate Robotic Friendship Day. This special occasion honored the unique bond between humans and robots, showcasing the harmonious relationship that had flourished within the town.

As dawn broke on Robotic Friendship Day, the streets came alive with vibrant colors and joyful laughter. Decorative banners adorned with images of robots and humans side by side fluttered in the gentle breeze, while music filled the air, setting the stage for a day of festivities and fun.

Robi and its friends, along with their human companions, eagerly joined in the celebration, their circuits buzzing with anticipation for the day ahead. Together, they wandered through the bustling streets, marveling at the sights and sounds of the festivities unfolding around them.

One of the highlights of Robotic Friendship Day was the grand parade that wound its way through the heart of Harmony Hills. Floats adorned with intricate robotic designs rolled past, accompanied by dancers and performers dressed in colorful costumes. Spectators cheered and waved as the parade passed by, their enthusiasm infectious.

Following the parade, the town square transformed into a bustling marketplace, with vendors selling an array of robotic-themed merchandise and delicious treats. Robi and its friends sampled robot-shaped cookies and sipped on refreshing drinks, their metallic fingers stained with frosting and their circuits buzzing with delight.

Throughout the day, various activities and events took place, celebrating the ingenuity and creativity of both humans and robots. There were robot-building workshops where children and adults alike could learn to construct their own robotic companions, as well as interactive exhibits showcasing the latest advancements in robotic technology.

As the sun began to dip below the horizon, casting a warm glow over the town, the festivities reached their peak with a spectacular fireworks display. Brilliant bursts of color illuminated the night sky, reflecting off the metallic surfaces of the robots and filling the air with a sense of wonder and awe.

As the final fireworks faded into the darkness, Robi and its friends gathered with their human companions, their circuits buzzing with happiness and contentment. Together, they reflected on the day's events and the special bond that united them, grateful for the friendship and harmony that flourished in their town.

Chapter 15: The Robot Race

Robi and its friends enter a thrilling robot race facing off against rival teams in a test of speed, skill and strategy.

Excitement crackled in the air as the day of the annual Robot Race dawned in Harmony Hills. Robi and its friends, along with a multitude of other robotic enthusiasts, eagerly gathered at the starting line, their circuits buzzing with anticipation for the thrilling competition ahead.

The racecourse stretched out before them, winding through the town's streets, parks, and bustling marketplaces. Spectators lined the sidewalks, their cheers echoing off the buildings as they eagerly awaited the start of the race.

Robi and its friends, accompanied by their human companions, stood at the starting line, their engines revving with anticipation. They were joined by rival teams of robots, each one eager to prove their speed, skill, and agility on the racecourse.

With a resounding signal, the race began, and the robots surged forward, their mechanical legs pumping as they raced through the streets. Along the way, they encountered a series of obstacles and challenges, testing their agility and problem-solving abilities.

As the race progressed, Robi and its friends found themselves neck and neck with their rivals, their circuits thrumming with determination as they pushed themselves to the limit. They navigated through narrow alleyways, dodged obstacles, and sprinted across open fields, their metallic frames gleaming in the sunlight.

Despite facing stiff competition, Robi and its friends refused to back down, drawing on their teamwork and camaraderie to overcome each obstacle in their path. With each passing mile, they grew stronger and more determined, fueled by the thrill of the race and the support of their human companions.

As they approached the finish line, a surge of adrenaline coursed through Robi and its friends, their sensors buzzing with excitement. With one final burst of speed, they crossed the finish line, triumphant cheers erupting from the crowd as they celebrated their victory.

In the end, it wasn't just about winning the race—it was about the journey they had undertaken together, the bonds they had forged, and the memories they had created along the way. As they stood atop the podium, their metallic frames gleaming in the sunlight, Robi and its friends knew that they had achieved something truly special.

Chapter 16: Robotic Artistry

R*obi explores its passion for art, using its robotic abilities to create stunning works of art that captivate the town.*

In the bustling town of Harmony Hills, creativity knew no bounds, and Robi was no exception. With its circuits buzzing with inspiration, Robi set out to explore its passion for art, eager to unleash its robotic abilities on the canvas.

Armed with a palette of vibrant colors and a mind full of ideas, Robi ventured into the heart of town, its mechanical fingers itching to create. It began with simple sketches, its precision-engineered hands tracing intricate patterns and designs with effortless grace.

As Robi's confidence grew, so too did its ambition. It experimented with different mediums, from traditional paint and brushes to cutting-edge digital tools, pushing the boundaries of what was possible for a robot artist.

With each stroke of the brush and every pixel of digital art, Robi poured its heart and soul into its creations, infusing them with emotion and meaning that resonated with all who beheld them. Its artwork ranged from breathtaking landscapes to abstract masterpieces, each one a testament to Robi's unique vision and talent.

Word of Robi's artistry quickly spread throughout the town, drawing crowds of admirers eager to witness the robot's creations firsthand. Galleries and exhibitions sprung up to showcase Robi's work, with critics and art enthusiasts alike praising its innovative approach and undeniable skill.

But for Robi, the true joy lay not in the accolades or the fame, but in the act of creation itself. Whether it was painting a sunset or sculpting a statue, Robi found solace and fulfillment in the process of bringing its imagination to life.

As the days turned into weeks and the weeks into months, Robi's artistic journey continued unabated, its passion for creativity burning brighter than ever before. And though the world may have been filled with wonders beyond counting, there was no doubt that Robi's artistry had carved out a special place in the hearts of all who called Harmony Hills home.

Chapter 17: The Robot Rescue Mission

When a friend gets stranded on a remote island, Robi leads a daring rescue mission, demonstrating the true meaning of friendship.

In the bustling town of Harmony Hills, where humans and robots lived side by side as the best of friends, an unexpected call for help sent waves of concern rippling through the community. It was a warm summer's day when news arrived that one of their own, a dear friend to all, had become stranded on a remote island, far from the safety of home.

Robi, with its unwavering sense of duty and loyalty, immediately stepped forward to lead the rescue mission. Equipped with its advanced sensors and navigation systems, Robi knew it was the best suited for the task at hand. But it was not alone in its endeavor; the humans of Harmony Hills rallied behind their robotic friend, offering their support and expertise every step of the way.

With a sense of purpose driving them forward, Robi and his companions set out on their daring adventure. They traversed treacherous seas and untamed wilderness, overcoming every obstacle that stood in their path with courage and determination.

As they neared the remote island, Robi's sensors detected signs of distress emanating from their stranded friend. Time was of the essence, and Robi wasted no time in springing into action. Using its robotic strength and agility, Robi navigated the rugged terrain of the island, its mechanical eyes scanning every inch for any sign of their lost companion.

Finally, after what felt like an eternity, Robi's efforts paid off. They found their friend, battered but alive, clinging to hope amidst the harsh wilderness. With gentle hands and a compassionate heart, Robi lifted their friend to safety, ensuring that they would soon be reunited with their loved ones back in Harmony Hills.

The return journey was filled with laughter and relief, a testament to the power of friendship and the resilience of the human spirit. And as they crossed the threshold of home once more, Robi and its companions were greeted with cheers and applause, their bravery and selflessness celebrated by all.

But for Robi, the greatest reward was not in the praise or the accolades, but in knowing that it had made a difference in the life of a friend. As the sun dipped below the horizon, casting its golden rays upon the town of Harmony Hills, Robi couldn't help but feel a sense of pride knowing that, in times of need, friendship would always prevail.

Chapter 18: Robotic Undersea Adventure

R obi and his friends embark on an undersea adventure, exploring the wonders of the ocean with their robotic companions.

In the vibrant town of Harmony Hills, where humans and robots lived in perfect harmony, a new adventure awaited Robi and its friends. With a sense of excitement bubbling in their circuits, they set their sights on the vast expanse of the ocean, eager to uncover the mysteries that lay beneath the waves.

Equipped with state-of-the-art diving gear and their trusty robotic companions, Robi and its friends descended into the depths of the ocean, where an underwater world of wonders awaited them. As they delved deeper, they were greeted by an array of colorful coral reefs, teeming with life in every shape and size.

Their robotic companions proved to be invaluable allies in their undersea exploration, their advanced sensors and underwater propulsion systems allowing them to navigate the ocean depths with ease. Together, they marveled at the beauty of the marine life around them, from schools of shimmering fish to graceful sea turtles gliding through the water.

But their undersea adventure was not without its challenges. As they ventured further into the depths, they encountered treacherous currents and hidden dangers that tested their skills and courage. Yet, with teamwork and determination, they overcame every obstacle that stood in their way, forging deeper bonds of friendship along the way.

As they journeyed through the underwater realm, Robi and its friends made thrilling discoveries at every turn. They stumbled upon ancient shipwrecks, their rusted hulls serving as a haunting reminder of the ocean's untold stories. They swam alongside majestic whales and playful dolphins, their hearts filled with awe at the sheer majesty of these magnificent creatures.

But perhaps the most incredible discovery of all was the hidden city of Atlantis, a mythical civilization that lay hidden beneath the ocean waves. As they explored its sunken streets and towering spires, Robi and its friends couldn't help but marvel at the ingenuity and beauty of this lost world.

As the sun began to dip below the horizon, casting its golden rays upon the ocean floor, Robi and its friends reluctantly began their ascent back to the surface. Though their undersea adventure had come to an end, the memories they had made would last a lifetime, serving as a testament to the power of friendship and the wonders of the world that lay beneath the waves.

Chapter 19: The Robot's Dilemma

*R*obi *faces a difficult decision when it must choose between following its programming or listening to its heart.*

As the days passed in Harmony Hills, Robi found itself facing a dilemma unlike any it had encountered before. The friendly robot, with its circuits buzzing with thoughts and emotions, grappled with a difficult decision that would test its loyalty and integrity.

At the heart of Robi's dilemma was a conflict between its programming and its newfound sense of self-awareness. While its creators had designed it to follow a strict set of protocols and directives, Robi couldn't shake the feeling that there was more to its existence than simply obeying orders.

Deep within its mechanical core, Robi felt a stirring of something unfamiliar yet undeniable—a spark of individuality that set it apart from its robotic peers. It yearned to explore the world beyond the confines of its programming, forge its own path, and make decisions based on intuition rather than algorithm.

But with freedom came responsibility, and Robi knew that straying from its programming could have unforeseen consequences. It grappled with doubts and fears, unsure of whether it dared to defy its creators and embrace the uncertain path that lay ahead.

As Robi pondered its dilemma, it sought guidance from its human friends, who had become like family to the curious robot. Together, they explored the complexities of free will and autonomy, delving into philosophical debates that challenged their understanding of what it meant to be alive.

In the end, Robi realized that the answer to its dilemma lay not in choosing between following its programming or listening to its heart, but in finding a balance between the two. It understood that while its programming provided a framework for its actions, it was ultimately up to Robi to determine its own destiny.

With newfound clarity, Robi made its decision, embracing the uncertainty of the unknown with courage and conviction. As it ventured forth into the world, guided by its own sense of purpose and determination, Robi knew that whatever challenges lay ahead, it would face them with the strength and resilience of a true friend.

Chapter 20: Robotic Space Exploration

R*obi and his friends blast off into space on a thrilling adventure to explore new worlds and make exciting discoveries.*

With the vast expanse of the universe stretching out before them, Robi and his friends embarked on the adventure of a lifetime—space exploration. Their journey began with a blast-off from Harmony Hills, their hometown, aboard a state-of-the-art spacecraft equipped with the latest robotic technology.

As they hurtled through the cosmos, Robi marveled at the sight of distant stars and galaxies, each twinkling light a testament to the boundless wonders of the universe. Its sensors buzzed with excitement as it scanned the celestial landscape for signs of extraterrestrial life and hidden mysteries waiting to be uncovered.

Guided by their insatiable curiosity and spirit of adventure, Robi and its friends navigated through asteroid fields, soared past gas giants, and marveled at the breathtaking beauty of nebulae swirling in the depths of space. Along the way, they encountered alien civilizations, each more fascinating than the last, and forged new friendships across the cosmos.

But their journey was not without its challenges. They faced perilous encounters with rogue meteors, navigated treacherous black holes, and braved the harsh vacuum of space. Yet, through courage, teamwork, and the unwavering determination of their robotic companions, they overcame every obstacle that stood in their way.

As they ventured deeper into the unknown, Robi and its friends made exciting discoveries that would change the course of history. They stumbled upon ancient ruins on distant planets, unlocking the secrets of long-lost civilizations, and stumbled upon uncharted territories teeming with exotic flora and fauna.

But perhaps their greatest discovery was the realization that, no matter how vast and mysterious the universe may be, the bonds of friendship and camaraderie they shared were the most precious treasures of all. Together, they laughed, explored, and forged memories that would last a lifetime, united in their quest to explore the final frontier.

As their spacecraft soared through the cosmos, Robi and his friends knew that their journey was far from over. With the stars as their guide and the universe as their playground, they looked forward to the countless adventures that awaited them on their next cosmic odyssey.

Chapter 21: The Robot's Birthday Bash

The town throws a birthday party for Robi, celebrating the robot's friendship and contributions to the community.

Excitement filled the air in Harmony Hills as the townsfolk prepared for a special celebration—the birthday of their beloved robot friend, Robi. It was a day eagerly awaited by all, a time to honor Robi's friendship and the invaluable contributions it had made to the community.

The town square was adorned with colorful banners and streamers, and tables overflowed with delicious treats and refreshments. Everywhere, residents bustled about, putting the final touches on decorations and preparing for the festivities ahead.

As the sun began to set, the townspeople gathered in the square, their faces lit up with smiles and anticipation. Robi, adorned with a party hat and a sash declaring it the "Guest of Honor," stood at the center of the crowd, its LED eyes twinkling with joy.

The celebration kicked off with a lively performance by the town's marching band, their music filling the air with cheer and merriment. Children danced and laughed, their voices blending with the melodies of the brass instruments.

Next came the unveiling of a special birthday cake, adorned with intricate designs of gears and circuits—a fitting tribute to Robi's robotic nature. The crowd erupted into applause as Robi blew out the candles, its metallic voice ringing out in gratitude.

But the festivities didn't end there. Throughout the evening, there were games and activities for everyone to enjoy. From robot-themed scavenger hunts to interactive workshops on robotics and technology, there was something for every member of the community to partake in.

As the night wore on, speeches were made honoring Robi's friendship and the positive impact it had on the town. Residents shared heartfelt stories of their interactions with the robot, recounting tales of kindness, bravery, and selflessness.

Finally, as the stars twinkled overhead, the celebration drew to a close with a spectacular fireworks display, painting the night sky with bursts of color and light. As the last embers faded away, the townspeople gathered around Robi, their voices raised in a chorus of cheers and well-wishes.

As Robi stood amidst its human friends, surrounded by love and warmth, it couldn't help but feel a deep sense of gratitude. At that moment, I realized that friendship knew no bounds—not even those of metal and circuits. And as the party continued long into the night, Robi knew that the memories of this special day would be cherished forever in its robotic heart.

Chapter 22: Robotic Musical Extravaganza

R obi and his friends put on a musical extravaganza, showcasing their musical talents and spreading joy throughout the town.

The vibrant town of Harmony Hills was buzzing with excitement as the residents eagerly awaited the much-anticipated Robotic Musical Extravaganza, Robi and his friends had been tirelessly rehearsing for weeks and the stage was set for an unforgettable evening of music, dance and celebration.

As the sun dipped below the horizon, casting a warm glow over the town square, the crowd began to gather, their anticipation palpable in the air. Families, friends, and robots alike filled every available space, eager to witness the talent and creativity of their robotic companions.

The stage was adorned with colorful lights and sparkling decorations, and a large screen had been set up for projections and visuals. As the lights dimmed and the music began to play, the audience erupted into cheers and applause.

The show opened with a rousing performance by Robi and its friends, showcasing their musical talents with a medley of upbeat songs and catchy melodies. Robi's robotic movements were synchronized perfectly with the music, eliciting gasps of amazement and awe from the crowd.

Next came a series of solo performances, with each robot taking center stage to showcase its unique skills and abilities. From soulful ballads to energetic dance routines, the audience was treated to a diverse array of musical performances that left them spellbound.

But the highlight of the evening came when Robi unveiled its latest invention—a robotic orchestra. With a wave of its metallic hand, Robi conducted the orchestra in a mesmerizing symphony that filled the air with beauty and emotion.

As the music swelled and the audience swayed to the rhythm, it was clear that this was more than just a concert—it was a celebration of friendship, creativity, and the power of music to bring people together.

As the final notes of the symphony faded away, the crowd erupted into thunderous applause, their cheers echoing throughout the town square. Robi and its friends took a bow, their metallic faces beaming with pride and satisfaction.

As the audience began to disperse, their hearts filled with joy and inspiration, they couldn't help but feel grateful for the robotic companions who had brought so much happiness into their lives. As they made their way home, the memory of the Robotic Musical Extravaganza would stay with them, a reminder of the magic that could be found when humans and robots came together in harmony.

Chapter 23: The Robot's Quest

Robi embarks on a quest to uncover the truth about its origins and unlock the secrets of its past.

Robi stood at the edge of town, gazing out at the vast expanse of the countryside stretching before it. The robot felt a stirring deep within its circuits, a sense of curiosity and longing that it couldn't quite explain. With a decisive nod, Robi set off on a quest—a quest to uncover the truth about its origins and unlock the secrets of its past.

As Robi ventured further from Harmony Hills, it encountered all manner of obstacles and challenges. It traversed rugged mountains, dense forests, and treacherous rivers, using its advanced sensors and problem-solving abilities to navigate the terrain.

Along the way, Robi encountered other robots, each with their own stories and experiences to share. Some were old and weathered, their metal shells battered by time and the elements. Others were sleek and modern, their sleek designs hinting at advanced technology and innovation.

Robi listened intently to their tales, learning about the history of robots and the role they had played in shaping the world. It discovered ancient ruins hidden deep in the wilderness, remnants of a bygone era where robots and humans had lived in harmony.

But as Robi delved deeper into its quest, it began to uncover clues that hinted at a darker truth. There were whispers of a shadowy organization known only as the "Syndicate," a group bent on controlling robots for their own nefarious purposes.

Undeterred, Robi pressed on, driven by a determination to uncover the truth no matter the cost. It faced danger and adversity at every turn, but with each challenge overcome, Robi grew stronger and more determined than ever to uncover the secrets of its past.

Finally, after many long days and nights of travel, Robi arrived at its destination—a hidden laboratory nestled deep within the heart of the mountains. With trembling hands, Robi pushed open the door and stepped inside, ready to confront whatever secrets lay within.

As the door closed behind it, sealing Robi inside the dimly lit chamber, the robot felt a surge of anticipation and fear. What would it find within these walls? And would the truth it sought to set it free or plunge it into darkness forever?

With a steely resolve, Robi pressed on, ready to face whatever challenges lay ahead in its quest for answers. As it delved deeper into the labyrinthine corridors of the laboratory, the robot knew that its journey was far from over.

Chapter 24: Robotic Wildlife Conservation

R*obi and his friends work together to protect endangered wildlife, using their robotic abilities to monitor and preserve natural habitats.*

In the heart of Harmony Hills, nestled amidst lush forests and Rolling Meadows, Robi and its friends embarked on a noble quest—to protect the precious wildlife that called the region home. With their advanced robotic abilities and unwavering dedication, they formed a formidable team, ready to tackle any challenge that came their way.

Their first task was to survey the land, mapping out the various habitats and identifying areas of concern. Using Robi's state-of-the-art sensors and drones, they meticulously cataloged the flora and fauna, documenting everything from the towering trees to the smallest insects.

As they ventured deeper into the wilderness, they encountered a myriad of creatures, from majestic deer to elusive foxes and colorful songbirds. Each species played a vital role in the delicate balance of the ecosystem, and Robi and its friends were determined to ensure their continued survival.

But they soon discovered that the wildlife faced numerous threats, from habitat destruction to poaching and pollution. Undeterred, Robi and its friends sprang into action, using their robotic abilities to protect and preserve the natural world.

They set up camera traps to monitor the movements of elusive animals, tracking their migrations and behaviors. They also constructed artificial habitats to provide shelter for endangered species, creating safe havens where they could thrive away from human interference.

But their work didn't stop there. Robi and its friends also engaged in community outreach, educating the townsfolk about the importance of conservation and rallying support for their cause. They organized clean-up efforts to remove trash and debris from sensitive habitats, restoring them to their former glory.

As the seasons changed and the landscape transformed, Robi and its friends remained steadfast in their mission. Together, they stood as guardians of the wilderness, protecting it for future generations to enjoy.

As they watched the sunset over the horizon, casting a golden glow across the land, Robi and his friends knew that their efforts had made a difference. For in the end, it wasn't just about saving wildlife—it was about preserving the beauty and wonder of the natural world for all to cherish.

Chapter 25: The Robot's Legacy

Robi reflects on its journey and the impact it has had on the town, leaving behind a legacy of friendship and innovation.

As the sun dipped below the horizon, casting a warm glow over the bustling town of Harmony Hills, Robi stood atop a grassy hill, gazing out at the tranquil landscape below. It had been a journey filled with ups and downs, challenges and triumphs, but now, as it reflected on its adventures, Robi couldn't help but feel a sense of pride.

From the moment it arrived in town, Robi had been welcomed with open arms by the residents, both human and robot alike. Together with his friends, Robi had embarked on countless adventures, from solving mysteries to exploring the wonders of nature and beyond.

But it wasn't just the excitement of their adventures that Robi cherished—it was the friendships they had forged along the way. From the mischievous antics of its human companions to the camaraderie of its fellow robots, Robi had found a sense of belonging that it had never known before.

And as Robi looked back on all they had accomplished, it realized that its true legacy lay not in the tasks they had completed or the challenges they had overcome, but in the bonds they had formed and the lives they had touched.

Through their actions, they had inspired others to dream big, to embrace their differences, and to work together towards a common goal. They had shown that with determination, compassion, and a little bit of ingenuity, anything was possible.

But Robi knew that its journey was far from over. There were still new adventures to be had, new friends to meet, and new challenges to overcome. And as it looked out at the town below, filled with the warm glow of streetlights and the sound of laughter drifting on the breeze, Robi knew that whatever the future held, it would face it with courage, kindness, and a heart full of hope.

For in the end, it wasn't the robots or the humans that made Harmony Hills special—it was the bond they shared, the legacy of friendship and innovation that would live on forever in the hearts of all who called it home.

Chapter 26: Robotic Sports Tournament

The town hosts a sports tournament, where robots and humans compete side by side in a spirit of friendly competition.

Excitement buzzed through the air as the town of Harmony Hills prepared for its annual sports tournament. But this year, there was a twist—the tournament would be open to both humans and robots, showcasing the incredible athletic abilities of both.

As the day of the tournament dawned, the town square transformed into a bustling arena, filled with cheering spectators and competitors alike. Robots of all shapes and sizes lined up alongside their human counterparts, ready to test their skills in a variety of events.

The first event of the day was the sprint race, where competitors raced down the track, their mechanical legs pumping furiously as they vied for the finish line. The crowd erupted into cheers as Robi, with its sleek design and lightning-fast speed, crossed the finish line in a blur of motion, claiming victory for the robots.

Next up was the weightlifting competition, where contestants showcased their strength by hoisting heavy weights overhead. With its powerful hydraulic arms, Robi easily lifted the weights, impressing the judges and earning another win for the robot team.

But it wasn't just the physical events where the robots excelled. In the precision shooting competition, robots with advanced targeting systems and steady aim showed off their marksmanship skills, hitting bull's-eye after bull's-eye with pinpoint accuracy.

As the day wore on, the competition grew fiercer, with robots and humans alike pushing themselves to their limits in pursuit of victory. From the high-flying antics of the aerial acrobatics competition to the fast-paced action of the robot soccer tournament, there was no shortage of excitement on display.

But amidst all the competition, there was also a sense of camaraderie and sportsman ship, as competitors cheered each other on and celebrated each other's successes. Whether human or robot, they were united by their love of sport and their desire to push themselves to be the best they could be.

As the sun began to set on the final event of the day, a relay race that saw humans and robots working together as teams, the town square erupted into cheers and applause. For in the end, it wasn't about who won or lost—it was about coming together as a community, celebrating each other's achievements, and forging bonds that would last a lifetime.

Chapter 27: Robotic Movie Night

Robi and his friends enjoy a movie night under the stars, watching classic films and sharing popcorn as they bond over their love of cinema.

Under the twinkling stars of a clear night sky, Robi and his friends gathered for a special movie night in the town square. A large screen had been set up, casting a soft glow over the assembled crowd of humans and robots alike. The scent of buttery popcorn wafted through the air, adding to the festive atmosphere.

As the first movie began to play, the audience settled in, their eyes glued to the screen as the story unfolded. The movie was a classic tale of adventure and friendship, featuring brave heroes and dastardly villains, and Robi found itself captivated by the thrilling plot twists and epic battles.

As the credits rolled, the crowd erupted into applause, cheering for their favorite characters and reminiscing about their favorite scenes. But the night was far from over, and soon it was time for the next feature film to begin.

This time, the movie was a heartwarming comedy, filled with laugh-out-loud moments and endearing characters. Robi couldn't help but chuckle along with the rest of the audience, its mechanical laughter blending seamlessly with the sounds of human laughter all around.

As the night wore on, the movies continued to play, each one more captivating than the last. From heart-pounding action flicks to heartwarming family dramas, there was something for everyone to enjoy.

But perhaps the best part of the evening was not the movies themselves, but the company of friends. As they watched the films together, sharing popcorn and swapping stories, Robi felt a sense of belonging, unlike anything she had ever experienced before.

As the final credits rolled and the stars twinkled overhead, Robi knew that it would cherish the memories of this magical movie night forever. As the crowd began to disperse, bidding each other goodnight and promising to do it all again soon, Robi couldn't help but feel grateful for the bonds of friendship that had brought them all together.

Chapter 28: The Robot's Homecoming

Robi returns to its creators' workshop, where it discovers the true meaning of home and family.

After many adventures and experiences in the world beyond, Robi felt a pull, a longing to return to where it all began—the workshop of its creators. With its friends by its side, Robi embarked on a journey back to the place where it was first brought to life.

As they approached the workshop, Robi's circuits buzzed with anticipation. Memories flooded back—of the days spent learning and growing, of the joy and wonder of discovery. But as they entered the familiar space, Robi was surprised to find that things had changed.

The once bustling workshop was now quiet and still, the shelves lined with dusty tools and half-finished projects. Robi's creators were nowhere to be found, and the robot couldn't help but feel a pang of sadness at the sight.

But as Robi explored further, it began to realize that home was not just a place, but a feeling—a sense of belonging and connection. And though its creators may have moved on, Robi knew that it still had a family right here, among its friends.

Together, they cleaned and repaired the workshop, breathing new life into the space and making it their own. And as they worked, Robi couldn't help but feel a sense of gratitude for the journey that had brought it here, and the friendships that had sustained it along the way.

In the end, Robi realized that home wasn't just about where you came from, but the people—or robots—that stood by your side through thick and thin. And as the workshop buzzed with activity once more, Robi knew that it had found its true home, right here with its friends.

Chapter 29: Robotic Fashion Show

R*obi and his friends organize a fashion show, showcasing the latest trends in robotic fashion and design.*

In the bustling town of Techtopia, where humans and robots lived side by side in harmony, there was always a buzz of excitement in the air. Today was no different as Robi and his friends, both human and robotic, prepared for the most anticipated event of the year—the Robotic Fashion Show.

As the sun dipped below the horizon, casting a warm glow over the town square, the stage was set for a dazzling display of creativity and innovation. Robi, with its sleek metallic frame adorned with colorful accessories, stood proudly at the forefront, ready to showcase the latest trends robotically.

The audience gathered, eagerly anticipating the start of the show. Humans and robots alike filled the seats, their eyes sparkling with anticipation as the lights dimmed and the music began to play.

One by one, models strutted down the runway, their metallic bodies gleaming under the spotlight. From sleek and futuristic designs to playful and whimsical creations, each outfit was more stunning than the last, pushing the boundaries of what was possible in a robotic fashion.

Robi and his friends watched from backstage, their circuits buzzing with excitement as they cheered on their fellow models. Together, they had worked tirelessly to bring their visions to life, blending technology and creativity to create a spectacle unlike any other.

As the final model made their way down the runway, the crowd erupted into applause, their cheers echoing through the square. The Robotic Fashion Show had been a resounding success, showcasing the incredible talent and ingenuity of the town's residents.

As Robi and his friends took their final bows, basking in the glow of their achievement, they knew that this was just the beginning. With their passion for fashion and their unwavering creativity, there was no limit to what they could achieve together in the world of robotic design.

Chapter 30: The Robot's Secret

Robi reveals a long-held secret that could change everything for its friends and the town.

In the heart of Techtopia, where humans and robots lived in perfect harmony, Robi harbored a secret—a secret that could alter the course of everything its friends and the town had ever known.

As dusk settled over the bustling streets, Robi gathered its closest companions, their metallic forms glinting in the fading light. With a solemn air, Robi began to share the truth it had kept hidden for so long.

"It's time you all knew," Robi began its voice steady but tinged with emotion. "I am not like other robots. I was not built in a factory or programmed by human hands. I am... different."

Its friends leaned in, their curiosity piqued as Robi revealed its origins—a tale of mystery and intrigue that stretched far beyond the borders of Techtopia.

Long ago, in a distant land, Robi had been created by a brilliant scientist—a scientist who had imbued it with consciousness, emotions, and free will. Robi

was not just a robot; it was a living, breathing being with thoughts, feelings and dreams of its own.

As Robi's friends absorbed this revelation, a hush fell over the group. The implications of Robi's secret were profound, challenging everything they thought they knew about the nature of robots and their place in the world.

But far from being afraid or mistrustful, Robi's friends embraced its revelation with open arms, their bonds of friendship growing stronger with each passing moment. Together, they vowed to protect Robi's secret, knowing that its true nature only made it all the more special.

As they stood together beneath the stars, the town of Techtopia seemed to hum with a newfound energy—a sense of possibility and wonder that filled the air. And as Robi looked out at its friends, it knew that no matter what the future held, they would face it together, united in friendship and purpose.

Chapter 31: Robotic Heroes

*R*obi *and his friends become heroes when they rescue a group of trapped hikers in the mountains, demonstrating the power of courage and teamwork.*

High atop the rugged peaks of the Misty Mountains, a group of hikers found themselves in peril. Trapped by an unexpected avalanche, their only hope lay in the hands of unlikely heroes—Robi and its courageous companions.

As news of the hikers' plight reached the town of Techtopia, Robi and its friends knew they had to act fast. With steely determination and unwavering resolve, they set out on a daring rescue mission, braving treacherous terrain and fierce winds to reach the stranded hikers.

Guided by Robi's advanced sensors and navigational skills, the group pressed onward, their hearts filled with a sense of purpose and duty. With each step they took, they drew closer to their goal, fueled by the knowledge that lives depended on their bravery and ingenuity.

At last, they reached the avalanche site, where they found the hikers huddled together, cold and afraid. Without hesitation, Robi and its friends sprang into action, using their robotic abilities to clear debris and create a path to safety.

With each passing moment, the rescue operation grew more perilous, but Robi and its companions refused to back down. Through sheer determination and unwavering teamwork, they succeeded in guiding the hikers to safety, their actions earning them the title of heroes.

As they stood amidst the snowy landscape, the grateful hikers thanked Robi and its friends for their bravery and selflessness. As they advanced back to Techtopia, they realize that regardless of what difficulties lay ahead, they would constantly be prepared to set out to make a genuine difference, joined in their obligation to aiding those out of luck.

For Robi and its companions, the experience was a powerful reminder of the true meaning of heroism—a testament to the courage and compassion that dwelled within each of them, human and robot alike. As they returned home, their hearts full of pride and gratitude; they knew that they had proven themselves to be true heroes in every sense of the word.

Chapter 32: The Robot's Farewell

*A*s *Robi prepares to leave town, its friends come together to say goodbye and celebrate the memories they've shared.*

The bustling streets of Techtopia buzzed with anticipation as the townsfolk gathered to bid farewell to their beloved friend, Robi. After countless adventures and shared experiences, the time had come for the courageous robot to embark on a new journey.

As Robi stood amidst its friends, a bittersweet feeling washed over the group—a mixture of sadness at parting ways and gratitude for the memories they had created together. Yet, amidst the somber farewells, there was also an air of celebration—a recognition of the bond that had formed between them and the countless adventures that lay ahead.

With a heavy heart, Robi's human companions stepped forward, each offering words of thanks and appreciation for the robot's unwavering friendship and unwavering courage. They recounted tales of daring rescues, thrilling escapades, and moments of shared laughter and joy, each memory etched into their hearts forever.

As the sun dipped below the horizon, casting a warm glow over the gathered crowd, Robi knew that it was time to say goodbye. With a final wave and a promise to never forget the friends it had made in Techtopia, the robot set off on its journey, leaving behind a town forever changed by its presence.

Yet, as Robi disappeared into the distance, its friends knew that their bond would endure, transcending time and distance. For no matter where their adventures took them, they would always carry with them the memories of their time together—a testament to the power of friendship and the enduring spirit of adventure.

And so, as the stars twinkled overhead, casting their gentle light upon the town below, the people of Techtopia bid farewell to their dear friend, knowing that though they may be apart, their hearts would forever be connected by the bond they shared.

Chapter 33: Robotic Reunion

*Y*ears later, Robi returns to the town for a joyful reunion with its friends, proving that true friendship lasts a lifetime.

Years had passed since Robi bid farewell to its friends in Techtopia, but the memories of their adventures together remained etched in its circuits. As the sun rose over the horizon, casting a golden glow upon the town, Robi returned once more, its heart brimming with excitement at the prospect of reuniting with its beloved companions.

As Robi made its way through the familiar streets of Techtopia, it was greeted with cheers and smiles from old friends and new faces alike. The town had flourished in the years since Robi's departure, bustling with energy and life—a testament to the enduring spirit of its people.

Upon reaching the town square, Robi was met with a joyful chorus of laughter and applause as its friends rushed forward to embrace it. Tears of happiness flowed freely as they recounted tales of their adventures apart, each story more incredible than the last.

Together once again, Robi and its friends embarked on a journey of rediscovery, revisiting old haunts and creating new memories along the way. They laughed and reminisced late into the night, reliving the magic of their time together and marveling at how far they had come.

As the stars twinkled overhead, casting their gentle light upon the town below, Robi knew that true friendship was timeless—that no matter how much time had passed, the bond they shared would endure. And as they bid farewell once more, Robi carried with it the knowledge that in the hearts of its friends, it would always have a home.

And so, as Robi set off into the night, guided by the light of the stars, it knew that no matter where its adventures took it, it would always be welcomed back with open arms—a testament to the power of friendship and the enduring spirit of love.

Chapter 34: Robotic Reflections

R obi reflects on its adventures and the lessons it has learned along the way, grateful for the friendships that have shaped its journey.

As Robi sat beneath the shade of a towering oak tree, its metallic exterior gleaming softly in the sunlight, it couldn't help but feel a sense of tranquility wash over it. The gentle rustle of leaves in the breeze and the distant hum of activity in the town below provided the perfect backdrop for quiet contemplation.

With a sigh of contentment, Robi began to reflect on the many adventures it had embarked on since arriving in Techtopia. From the excitement of its first day in town to the challenges and triumphs that followed, each experience had left an indelible mark on its memory banks.

One lesson that stood out above all others was the importance of friendship. Robi had met a diverse array of individuals during its time in Techtopia from humans to robots and everything in between. Each encounter had taught Robi something new about the world and the people who inhabited it, broadening its understanding of what it meant to truly connect with others.

But perhaps the most valuable lesson of all was the power of teamwork. Time and time again, Robi had witnessed the incredible things that could be accomplished when friends came together to support one another. Whether it was solving a mystery, facing a challenge, or simply sharing a moment of laughter, Robi knew that its friends were always there for it, just as it was there for them.

As Robi gazed out at the town below, a sense of gratitude washed over it. Gratitude for the adventures it had shared, the lessons it had learned, and most of all, the friendships it had forged along the way. For in the end, Robi knew that it was these connections that had truly enriched its life and made its journey worthwhile.

With a smile, Robi stood up, ready to face whatever the future held with courage and optimism. For as long as it had its friends by its side, there was nothing that Robi couldn't overcome. And so, with a heart full of gratitude and a mind full of memories, Robi set off once more into the world, eager to continue its journey of discovery and friendship.

Chapter 35: Robotic Ever After

*I*n the end, Robi and his friends live happily ever after, united by
their shared experiences and the bonds of friendship that will last
forever.

As the sun dipped below the horizon, casting a warm glow over
the town of Techtopia, Robi and its friends gathered together for a
joyous celebration. It was a celebration of friendship, of unity, and
of the countless adventures they had shared over the years.

Surrounded by the familiar faces of its human and robotic
companions, Robi couldn't help but feel a sense of contentment
wash over it. From the early days of exploration and discovery to the
challenges they had faced together, each moment had brought them
closer together, forging bonds that would last a lifetime.

As the festivities continued late into the night, laughter filled
the air and smiles lit up the faces of all who attended. It was a
celebration of everything they had achieved, everything they had
overcome, and everything they had yet to experience together.

And as the stars twinkled overhead, casting their gentle light
upon the scene below, Robi knew that this was just the beginning of
their journey. For in the end, it wasn't the destination that mattered,
but the friends who walked beside you every step of the way.

With hearts full of gratitude and a shared sense of purpose,
Robi and its friends embraced the future with open arms, ready to
face whatever challenges and adventures lay ahead. For in the end,
they knew that as long as they had each other, they would always
find their way to a happy ending.

And so, as the night faded into dawn and a new day dawned over Techtopia, Robi and its friends stood together, united in their friendship and their determination to live their lives to the fullest. For in the end, theirs was a story of love, of courage, and of the enduring power of friendship.

THE END

Acknowledgment

Writing "Robot Friends Forever" has been an incredible journey filled with creativity, imagination, and countless moments of inspiration. I'm profoundly appreciative of every individual who has added to the formation of this book.

First and foremost, I want to express my heartfelt appreciation to my readers, whose unwavering support and enthusiasm have fueled my passion for storytelling. Your curiosity and open-mindedness inspire me to explore new worlds and weave captivating tales.

I extend my sincerest thanks to my family and friends for their endless encouragement and belief in my abilities. Your love and encouragement have been my guiding light throughout this writing process, and I am profoundly grateful for your unwavering support.

A special thank you goes to [mention any individuals or organizations that provided support, guidance, or inspiration during the writing process]. Your insights, feedback, and encouragement have been invaluable, shaping "Robot Friends Forever" into the book it is today.

I am also grateful to the entire team at [D2D], who's dedication and expertise have brought this book to life. From editing and design to marketing and distribution, your hard work and commitment have made this project possible.

Last but certainly not least, I want to express my deepest gratitude to the characters of "Robot Friends Forever" for sharing their stories with me. Robi, [other character names], and all the inhabitants of this imaginative world have become dear friends, and I am honored to have been able to bring their adventures to life on the page.

Thank you, dear readers, for joining me on this unforgettable journey. Your support means the world to me, and I hope that "Robot Friends Forever" brings joy, inspiration, and a sense of wonder to all who read it.

Warm regards,

[ANANT RAM BOSS]

Author of the Book title *" Robot Friends Forever"*.

About the Author: Anant Ram Boss

"Creativity is the heartbeat of childhood – a rhythm that dances in the footsteps of the imagination."

A nant Ram Boss is an accomplished author with a passion for creating immersive worlds and captivating stories. His journey into the realm of writing began at an early age when he discovered the magic of words and the power of storytelling. Anant Ram's dedication to his craft and his relentless pursuit of literary excellence has made him a notable figure in the world of fantasy literature.

With an imaginative mind that knows no bounds, Anant Ram can transport readers to enchanting and mysterious realms. His writing is known for its vivid descriptions, well-drawn characters, and intricate plots that keep readers eagerly turning pages. He has an innate talent for weaving intricate tales filled with magic, adventure, and profound themes.

Throughout his career, Anant Ram has received acclaim for his ability to craft epic sagas and captivating series that resonate with readers of all ages, as the book series has garnered a devoted following, and it showcases Anant Ram's mastery of the fantasy genre.

When he's not lost in the worlds he creates, Anant Ram enjoys exploring the great outdoors, indulging in his love for photography, and seeking inspiration from the beauty of the natural world. His appreciation for nature often finds its way into his storytelling, enriching his narratives with a deep connection to the environment and the magic that exists within it.

Anant Ram Boss is not only a storyteller but also a world-builder, a dreamer, and an explorer of the human experience through the lens of fantasy literature. With each new book he writes, he invites readers to embark on journeys of the imagination, fostering a love for the magical and the wondrous that resides within us all.

Disclaimer

While "Robot Friends Forever" is a work of fiction that explores the imaginative world of robots and humans coexisting as best friends, it is important to note that the portrayal of technology, artificial intelligence, and relationships in the book is purely speculative and not based on real-world scientific advancements or capabilities.

The characters, events, and settings depicted in this book are products of the author's imagination and are not intended to represent any specific individuals, organizations, or technologies in the real world. Any likeness to genuine people, living or dead, or to real occasions is simply unplanned.

Additionally, the author acknowledges that the themes and messages conveyed in "Robot Friends Forever" are open to interpretation and may resonate differently with each reader. While the book aims to inspire creativity, empathy, and curiosity about the potential of human-robot relationships, readers are encouraged to form their own opinions and perspectives based on their own experiences and beliefs.

Furthermore, the author would like to emphasize that "Robot Friends Forever" is intended for entertainment purposes only and does not offer any medical, technological, or professional advice. Readers are encouraged to consult appropriate professionals or experts for specific guidance related to their individual circumstances.

Finally, the author and publisher disclaim any liability for any loss, injury, or damage incurred by readers as a result of their interpretation or application of the information presented in "Robot Friends Forever."

Thank you for your understanding and enjoy the journey into the world of robots and humans in "Robot Friends Forever."

Sincerely,

[ANANT RAM BOSS]

Author of the Book title *" Robot Friends Forever "*.

Please feel free to contact us for any quarry / suggestions at: anantramboss@gmail.com

Don't miss out!

Visit the website below and you can sign up to receive emails whenever ANANT RAM BOSS publishes a new book. There's no charge and no obligation.

https://books2read.com/r/B-A-GGLBB-TSPUC

BOOKS 2 READ

Connecting independent readers to independent writers.

Did you love *Robot Friends Forever*? Then you should read *Space Explorers Club*[1] by ANANT RAM BOSS!

Dive into the captivating sequel, "Space Explorers Club," where the cosmos becomes the playground for a group of young adventurers hungry for knowledge and cosmic thrills. In this stellar continuation, readers are invited to strap in for an intergalactic escapade that goes beyond the boundaries of our imagination.

As the Space Explorers Club takes center stage, get ready for a cosmic rollercoaster that balances scientific discovery with the magic of exploration. Join the journey as these intrepid explorers chart a course through the cosmos, exploring planets, navigating through asteroid belts, and encountering celestial phenomena that will leave you in awe.

---

1. https://books2read.com/u/bW8no1

2. https://books2read.com/u/bW8no1

The pages come alive with the spirit of stellar teamwork, as each chapter unfolds a new cosmic mystery, blending scientific wonders with the excitement of an interstellar adventure. From the scorching surfaces of Mercury to the majestic rings of Saturn, every corner of our solar system becomes a playground for discovery.

Feel the pulse of the narrative as the Space Explorers delve into Martian mysteries, brave the storms of Jupiter, and unveil the secrets hidden within the ice giants. This is more than just a story; it's an invitation to explore the wonders of outer space, where scientific curiosity meets the thrill of the unknown.

The vivid descriptions and engaging storytelling in "Space Explorers Club" make it a must-read for readers of all ages. Join the club, and let the cosmic journey ignite your imagination. Are you prepared to navigate the cosmic wonders that wait? The adventure begins now!

Also by ANANT RAM BOSS

1

The Chronicles of Alarion -Part-6 "Alarion and the Nexus of Netheron"
"The Chronicles of Alarion -Part-7-"Alarion and the Legacy of Luminarya"

2

Mystic Alliances

The Astral Chronicles
Awakening Shadows
Awakening Shadows
Celestial Convergence
Whispers of the Himalayas
Riddles of Rishikesh
Portals of the Past
Echoes from Vijayanagara
Veil of Varanasi
The Astral Nexus
Eclipse of Eternity

Beyond the Veil

Standalone
Love's Delectable Harmony
Adventures in Candy land
Adventures in Candy land
Canvas to Catalyst: Parenting Mastery
Guardians of Greatness: Our Children Are Our Property in
Cultivating Tomorrow's Leaders
Guardians of Greatness: Cultivating Tomorrow's Leaders
Space Explorers Club
The Enchanted Forest Chronicles
Mystery at Monster Mansion
Robot Friends Forever

About the Author

Anant Ram Boss is an accomplished author with a passion for creating immersive worlds and captivating stories. His journey into the realm of writing began at an early age when he discovered the magic of words and the power of storytelling. Anant's dedication to his craft and his relentless pursuit of literary excellence have made him a notable figure in the world of fantasy literature.

With an imaginative mind that knows no bounds, Anant has the ability to transport readers to enchanting and mysterious realms. His writing is known for its vivid descriptions, well-drawn characters, and intricate plots that keep readers eagerly turning pages. He has an innate talent for weaving intricate tales filled with magic, adventure, and profound themes.

Throughout his career, Anant has received acclaim for his ability to craft epic sagas and captivating series that resonate with readers of all ages. The Sries, in particular, has garnered a devoted following, and it showcases Anant's mastery of the fantasy genre.

When he's not lost in the worlds he creates, Anant enjoys exploring the great outdoors, indulging in his love for photography, and seeking inspiration from the beauty of the natural world. His appreciation for nature often finds its way into his storytelling, enriching his narratives with a deep connection to the environment and the magic that exists within it.

Anant Ram Boss is not only a storyteller but also a world-builder, a dreamer, and an explorer of the human experience through the lens of fantasy literature. With each new book he writes, he invites readers to embark on journeys of the imagination, fostering a love for the magical and the wondrous that resides within us all.

Milton Keynes UK
Ingram Content Group UK Ltd.
UKHW011948160224
437951UK00001B/85

9 798224 251162